ARCHITECTURA

NAVALIS

AERONAUTICA

COLLECTED THOUGHTS ON THE

STEAMPUNK AIRSHIP

Contents

Introduction and Author's Note

It has been my intention to write a book on steampunk airships for some years now. While airships are a common feature across steampunk as a whole, very little has been written on the vessels themselves, and to my knowledge, no comprehensive text exists that focuses on them.

Given their large size, expense, and perhaps well founded safety concerns, it's not possible for the majority of us to own an airship or even to experience dirigible flight. For those of us then that love them, we must turn to books and other media instead to indulge our interest.

The subject is a much broader one than I initially realised. It was originally my intention just to include a brief summary of the physics of airship flight, followed by a short colour section featuring a selection of designs. In the event however, it has expanded to additionally include discussions of real world airship history, notes on fictional airship design, piracy and privateering, and even thoughts on the worlds in which these vessels fly.

It was also my intention to present this book as a fully academic discussion of the topic – again, my feelings on this have changed through the course of writing the book, and I think now it's more of an eclectic collection of thoughts. In a way, this suits the nature of steampunk! I do apologise though for switching between first and third person language in different chapters – I considered changing this, but ultimately I felt it better to leave this sections as-is and address the reader directly.

The name of the book has been based on that of a classic 18th Century codex on naval architecture – Fredrik Henrik af Chapman's *Architectura Navalis Mercatoria*. I have used the name previously for a series of talks given at the *Weekend at the Asylum* festival in Lincoln, and I felt that it would be fitting as something of a homage to the original text.

I hope then that you will find this book interesting – even if you disagree with my thoughts and opinions on the matter, I would be happy to see wider discussion of steampunk airships at events and online, and see more models and artworks presented at the same.

Matthew Slater
April 2018

STEAMPUNK & THE AIRSHIP

The airship is a machine that has been with steampunk since its very earliest days. They have appeared in a substantial number of steampunk novels, films, books, games and artworks, and form something of a staple of transport in the genre. The full literary origins of steampunk are beyond the bounds of this book, but it is worth mentioning that the earliest "full unashamed steampunk" literary reference to an airship, to the author's knowledge, is in the opening James Blaylock's 1986 novel Homunculus. Tim Power's *The Anubis Gates* and K.W. Jeter's *Moorlock Nights*, the other two "founding" steampunk novels don't feature airships explicitly.

Studio Ghibli's 1986 film *Laputa: Castle in the Sky* also has a distinctive steampunk aeronautical flavour – it's difficult to give it the full SP title, but its appearance at the same time as the first true steampunk novels and strong aesthetics makes it a key film in our story.

Of course, airships had appeared previously in proto-steampunk works of the likes of Michael Moorcock (The warlord of the air), and in the original Victorian/Edwardian science fiction novels of H.G. Wells (*The war in the air*) and Jules Verne (*Robur the Conqueror, Master of the world*) to name but a very few. Flight was something of an ultimate achievement to the Victorians, and it's no surprise that flying machines appeared in their science fictions.

Airships have continued to appear in steampunk works since – the list is too long to include here, but they've featured as everything from background details of the worlds in which the stories are set, through to almost full characters in their own right. Although difficult to quantify, the number of books that include them in some capacity seems to far exceed those that don't.

All of this begs the question – why are airships so intrinsic to steampunk? The answer to this can be found primarily in two things – the nature of the genre and the nature of people.

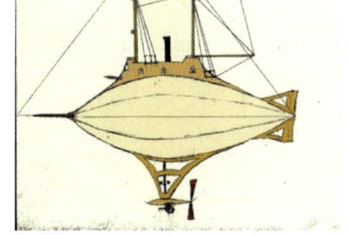

It's a cliche often repeated that mankind has dreamt of flight since its earliest days. Nonetheless, the desire to fly is strong in many of us. The strongly linked periods of the enlightenment, the industrial revolution and

the Victorian era that form the core inspiration for steampunk saw mankind's earliest flights. In the late 8th century the Montgolfier brothers flew their first hot air balloons, while Henri Giffard flew his steam-powered, coal gas filled airship in 1852 (the first successful powered flight – just about steerable in very calm weather). More advanced airship designs followed in the latter half of the 19th century, and culminated – just a year before Queen Victoria's death – with the flight of the rigid airship, LZ-1, in 1900. This was the very first "Zeppelin" that gave rise to the infamous bombers of the first world war, and later the passenger airliners of the 1930's, such as *Graf Zeppelin* and *Hindenburg*.

Things change rather dramatically at the end of this period – 1903, just two year's after Queen Victoria's death, saw the Wright brothers undertake the first heavier than air flight at Kitty Hawk, North Carolina. Airship development continued, but the aeroplane overtook it as the pre-eminent means of air transportation, and the airship is a rare sight today.

What this means, from our retro-futuristic persective – is that we have a technology that permitted human flight right in the middle of the period most drawn upon for steampunk, and which largely disapeared before the majority of us were born (I apologise to some of the older steampunks out there who may have been around late in that era – but what a marvellous connection to have!). This of course is very fertile ground for imagination. We dream as humans of flying, and we dream as steampunks of things we never could have experienced. We can't resist the airborne nostalgia of the airship.

The general (but not complete) disappearance of the dirigible from modern aviation lends itself to an interesting question - "What if the airship had become the main means of air travel". That line of thinking goes right to the heart of steampunk – how did the Victorians see the future?

Airships have a number of advantages over aeroplanes and helicopters in the world of fiction. To begin with, an airship doesn't require fuel to remain aloft – they fly in the same manner as a surface ship floats. This gives, in principal if not in reality, unlimited range to the

ship – a character aboard an airship can remain aloft in that world indefinitely, without the unconscious sense of the need to return to earth than an aeroplane gives.

Perhaps the main advantage from a retro-futuristic or historical standpoint is the subconscious connotations of the word "airship" itself. Aeronautical history, compared to nautical, is relatively short – two centuries or so, from the first balloon flight, as compared to around five millennia from the first known surface ships to now.

By associating the term "ship" with the aircraft, the author gains a strong mental link to the maritime world. Suddenly, the vessel needn't be just a machine – it can be a community, a means of exploration, or a man of war, with traditions, rituals, songs, food, heraldry, uniforms, and perhaps even a soul.

One advantage of this, and the time period in which steampunk is generally set, is that naval architecture changed dramatically through the 19th century – HMS Victory was typical of a large warship in 1805, and HMS Dreadnought state of the art in 1906. A steampunk airship can draw on pretty much anything in between or beyond – you can have a ship that evokes the days of Nelson and Trafalgar, or of Jellicoe and Jutland.

At the same time, it *is* still an aircraft – although shorter than marine, aeronautical history is incredibly bright and rich, with much to draw on. It to has its rituals and traditions, many of them common with marine, but many of them distinct – the traditional dress of a pilot for example is distinct from that of a sailor.

As a final point on the relationship between airships and steampunk, is the supposition that the airship is so intrinsic to the latter that it's inclusion in another context can make that world steampunk. For example, adding an advertsing blimp to a space opera wouldn't work in that regard – but adding a 1914 Zeppelin to a world of high fantasy could create a steam-fantasy world.

THE AIRSHIP AS A LITERARY DEVICE

Like many fictional ships, steampunk airships can fulfill a variety of roles in different stories. Rather than the purpose for which the ship was designed, this relates in this context to what part the ship plays in the character's journey. Many genres of fiction, from historical drama to space opera feature a ship of one type or another. Often, this just provide background to a world, or provide a means to an end for characters – the presence of a nameless cross channel steamer in a *Sherlock Holmes* story is hardly an important plot point, but gives a little colour nonetheless.

On the other hand, ships can also be key characters. In the Patrick O'Brians *Aubrey and Maturin* series of books (also known as *Master and Commander*), the Napoleonic frigate HMS *Surprise* is a recurring feature, and the reader swiftly grows attached to the vessel. Aside from the time the heroes of a story spend aboard a vessel, it's the features and faults of the vessel that give it character itself. HMS *Surprise* is a fairly old ship at the point at which she appears in the books, but her crew often find themselves triumphing over their foes despite her small size and ageing battery.

A good example, although more sci-fi than steampunk, comes from Joss Whedon's series *Firefly*. The key ship – *Serenity* – is a battered, ageing freighter, that's constantly breaking down. Few would argue however that the series would be the same without her. One reason for this perhaps is the bond between a captain and their ship. As has been mentioned before, a ship is a community, not just an object – without a ship, a captain is nothing. Therefore, if a reader cares about a captain as a character, they must also care about the ship.

Bringing things back around to steampunk airships, all of these points apply just the same. An airship can just be a background object, adding that note of flavour to a world – or it can be a character and setting in its own right. It's up to the artist or author to choose which, of course. Size does matter in this context – a very small airship is more akin to an aeroplane or helicopter than a surface ship in character, whereas something along the lines of the *Hindenburg* has something of the feel of an ocean liner about it.

Another point where an airship can be critical to a steampunk setting is in its engineering. Ships can often reflect the technological state of the art of a civilisation, especially in the 19th century, and this is equally true of the steampunk airship. A ship of any type has to be self sufficient for weeks or months at a time – carrying its own food, water and fuel, sheltering its crew, and even dealing with its own waste. It also has to be strong enough to withstand the forces of nature arrayed against it, capable of moving itself, and navigating. To meet these needs, a steampunk society must equip its airships with the very best it can in new innovations and devices. Perhaps a steam turbine for propulsion, an analytical engine to navigate, and the very newest and lightest allows for its structure.

What does this mean for a steampunk setting? An airship's role is not just what it does, or what sort of character it has in a story. It means that the level of technology carried on an airship sets a minimum level for technology in the fictional world in which it flies. It also helps set *when* the world is – or for alternative histories, helps illustrate deliberate anachronisms for the audience.

A Brief History of Dirigibles

Some of the history of balloons and airships has already been discussed in the previous chapter, but it's worth telling a brief version of the full story here. Although steampunk airships are by their nature fictional, the historical basis of the genre means a knowledge of their real-world origins is useful.

Pinning down a starting point for our history is difficult – even before the Montgolfier brother's first flight, concepts for flying machines had existed for centuries – Leonardo da Vinci's ornithopters, helicopter and gliders provide a famous example.

Later, in the 17th century, the Italian Jesuit Francesco Lana de Terzi proposed a "flying ship" carried aloft by four copper spheres, each containing a vacuum. Although the lifting principal was fundamentally sound, the spheres would have been crushed by air pressure as soon as the air inside was pumped out – however, the machine was an interesting step forwards and deserves inclusion here as a very early design of a lighter than air craft.

Skipping forward to the late 18th century, the Montgolfier brother's achievement with their hot air balloon demonstrated that human flight was possible – others swiftly followed suit with balloons of their own, using either hot air of hydrogen to provide lift. It was quickly realised that it would be very useful to make the balloons steerable in the air – or *dirigible*.

Many ideas were proposed to achieve this in the late 18th and earlier half of the 19th century – sails, aerial oars, even birds – but all were doomed to failure. What was needed was a a mechanical means of providing power - an engine.

The steam engine was likely first invented by the ancient Greek engineer Hero of Alexandria. His Aeolipile, was an early form of reaction turbine. Another invention used hot air to open and close temple doors – a primitive combustion engine. The modern steam engine has existed in recognisable form since Thomas Newcomen's pumping engine of 1712.

Early engines were of the atmospheric type, using ambient air pressure to push a piston against a vacuum created by condensing steam in the cylinder, and were too heavy to be truly practical for transportation use. While steam engine development is beyond the scope of this book, the engines were gradually improved through the 18th and 19th centuries with a range of innovations, such as the separate condenser and high pressure steam, followed by compounding and triple more expansion engines (using the steam in two or more cylinders) and eventually, in 1884, the steam turbine. The last three of these shall be covered in more detail in later chapters, but the development of the steam engine in general is a fascinating history that deserves greater study than the few lines given here.

Going back to the flying machine, in 1852, a French steam engine designer by the name of Henri Giffard built what is considered to be the first functioning airship. Fundamentally, it was his expertise in engine design that allowed him to produce a steam engine that was small and light enough to power a balloon. Giffard's ship has been mentioned previously, but the details bear repeating – it was a cigar shaped vessel 143 feet long, inflated with coal gas (a.k.a. town gas – the gas given off by heating coal in an airless environment), and powered by a three horsepower steam engine. He achieved a speed through the air of just over 5 knots, or 6 m.p.h – just enough to make the ship steerable in calm weather, but useless in adverse winds.

Development of the airship was slow through the latter half of the 19th century. Although Giffard had demonstrated that it was possible to build such a machine, the problem of finding an adequate prime mover still remained. Steam engines and their boilers are heavy, and have a low "power to weight ratio" - that is to say the power developed relative to the weight of the engine and boiler is generally poor; this is a huge issue for airships, where weight is critical to a successful design. Even with high pressure steam, a great improvement over the older atmospheric engines, the steam engine would never be a practical source if power for dirigibles in the 19th century.

What was required then was a better engine or motor. Experiments were made in France with electric motors in the latter part of the 19th century, and they were met with some success – in 1884, the 170ft non-rigid *La France* achieved a speed on its first flight of about 20 m.p.h. - enough to fight against the wind and critically, return to the point of starting.

Better still was to come in engine development – the internal combustion engine, free of the boiler that makes steam engines so heavy, was developed throughout the 19th century. By the 1880's they were finally coming of age, with the first cars being produced in 1886. All of the elements were ready for the creation of the first *practical* airships – what was needed was a man to combine them.

In step Alberto Santos-Dumont – this Franco-Brazilian inventor flew his first ship, *Number 1*, in 1898. The 83ft long hydrogen filled vessel utilised a small and light petrol engine, and demonstrated a degree of mobility hitherto unseen in an airship. Although the flight ended with a minor crash landing,

it showed the potential in combining an internal combustion engine with a balloon – and helped paved the way for further developments in the 20th century. Santos-Dumont continued to build airships for some years, becoming a celebrated figure in Parisian society during the latter years of the 19th century, before eventually switching his attentions to heavier than air flight. It's worth mentioning perhaps that Santos-Dumont wasn't the first to use an internal combustion engine in an airship – but he was the first to do it successfully.

Another great name appeared in the world of lighter than air flight around the turn of the 20th century – after a long period of fund raising and development, Ferdinand von Zeppelin's LZ-1 flew for the first time on the second of July, 1900. LZ-1 was set apart from the other early pioneers by virtue of her construction – rather than using the gas pressure inside the envelope to maintain the shape of the ship, LZ-1 was a rigid airship, using a framework of aluminium girders to support a series of lifting gas cells. This allows the construction of much larger vessels than their non rigid counterparts, and hence a greater carrying capacity. After a complicated series of events, including accidents, setbacks and twists of fate, the Zeppelin was a developed to a point where a passenger airline, DELAG (Deutsche Luftschiffahrts-Aktiengesellschaft) was in operation before the outbreak of the First World War.

At the turn of the 20th century then, it had been demonstrated that airship were a viable proposition. Development continued throughout the 1900's until in 1914, the airship faced the first severe test of its utility – that of the first world war.

As is often the case, the war acted as a catalyst for the development of technologies new and existing. Both the allied and central powers used airships during the first world war – most famously, the Zeppelin and the rival Schutte-Lanz rigids were used in the first strategic air raids against England, attacking targets from Lowestoft to London. Eventually, development of aeroplanes made these untenable, but significant panic was caused throughout the United Kingdom (and elsewhere) by these attacks.

Both sides also made of airships, including the smaller non-rigid ships, for scouting roles. The Zeppelins themselves were intended for use as the eyes of the German High Seas Fleet, while the Royal Naval Air Service successfully made use of the Sea-Scout, Coastal-Scout and North Sea class airships to patrol for U-Boats in the North Sea. It was in this role that the airship was found to be the most useful – too slow and vulnerable by the late war for use as a bomber, the long endurance of the airships made them perfect for maritime reconnaissance work – a role they reprised in the Battle of the Atlantic during the second world war.

During the interwar period, airship development continued across Europe and the U.S.A. The Italians built a number of semi-rigid airships – a halfway house between the rigid and non rigid types, with a structural keel helping to support the envelope above. This included Umberto Nobile's *Norge,* which undertook a flight across the north pole with the famed explorer Roald Amundsen in 1926.

In Germany, following the end of the war, the Zeppelin company (under Count Zeppelin's protégé and successor, Hugo Eckener) had been pushing for the return of a passenger airship service. Two commercial vessels (*Bodensee* and *Nordstern*) were built, but subsequently seized by the allies, along with the surviving wartime Zeppelins. These were divided amongst Great Britain, France and Italy, but not the U.S. – keen to acquire a Zeppelin, they took the surprising step of commissioning Eckener to build a vessel for the U.S Navy, in lieu of a substantial figure in war reparations. The resulting ship, LZ-126 Los Angeles, was completed in late 1924.

The German-American alliance continued through the interwar period, and a number of rigid ships were built for the U.S. Navy throughout the 1920's and 1930's - the *Shenandoah*, *Akron* and *Macon*. Sadly, all three of these vessels were also lost in storms during that period. These tragedies turned the U.S. Navy away from the rigid airship even before the much more dramatic loss of the *Hindenburg*.

USS *Akron* and USS *Macon*, the largest helium filled airships ever built, both had a distinctive design feature – they were flying aircraft carriers. Each could carry 3-5 F9C Sparrowhawk fighters, which were deployed via a hook from a hangar in the bottom of the ships. This feature was also to be found on the British rigid airship R33 – experiments were made, and eventually the vessel was able to launch and recover two Gloster Grebe biplanes. Her sister ship, R34, made the first east to west transatlantic crossing, shortly after Alcock and Brown made their pioneering transatlantic flight the other way in a Vickers Vimy bomber.

In the United Kingdom, experience with captured German Zeppelins led to the development a series of post war rigid airship – the R32, the R33 and R34 - which have been mentioned already - but of additional note was the R38. Like the LZ-126 *Los Angeles*, she was built for the U.S. Navy - however, before her delivery voyage, she suffered a serious structural failure and crashed with the loss of 44 of her crew. Some of the best and brightest in the British airship world were onboard at the time of the disaster, and their loss was a major setback to rigid airship development in the UK.

It took nearly a decade for airship building in Britain to fully recover, but eventually, in 1929, the rigid airships R100 and R101 took their first flights. Both vessels were designed to provide an air service to link the disparate arms of Empire, with the R100 designed by Dr Barnes Wallis (of bouncing

bomb fame) at Vickers, and the R101 by V.C. Richmond at the Royal Airship Works. The ships were assembled side by side in giant hangars at RAF Cardington, Bedfordshire.

R100, after initial teething problems, proved a successful ship – she made an impressive return flight to Canada in 1930. R101's fate was not so lucky – on her first flight to India in the same year, she crashed into a French hillside and exploded, killing the majority of the 54 people onboard. R100 was grounded after the disaster, and rigid airship development in the UK ended.

In Germany, the Los Angeles was followed in 1928 by perhaps the most successful of all the rigid airships – the LZ-127 *Graf Zeppelin*. Named in honour of the company's founder, she made a full circumnavigation in 1929, and enjoyed a successful career operating as an airliner between Germany and South America. She was eventually scrapped in 1937, having enjoyed nearly a full decade of successful operation.

Graf Zeppelin was succeeded, in 1936, by the most famous, or perhaps infamous of all the airships – LZ-129 *Hindenburg*. Her history hardly needs repeating here, but her loss to fire at Lakehurst, New Jersey in 1937 sounded a death knell for the rigid airship, and no further great rigid ships have been built since. The spectacular nature of the accident, captured on film, finally caused the public to lose faith in airships as a means of transportation. Some held out hope for a renaissance in airship travel following the end of the second world war, but by this point, the passenger airliner was coming of age and the world had changed, perhaps forever.

Hindenburg was followed by one final rigid Zeppelin airship – LZ-130 *Graf Zeppelin (II)*. Originally built as a passenger ship, the *Hindenburg* disaster the year before her first flight precluded this – she was used instead by the Nazi government on secret electronic reconnaissance flights along the East coast of England, to investigate a mysterious new line of radio towers. These would turn out to be for the "Chain Home" RADAR system, pivotal in the Battle of Britain.

Our story doesn't end there though – airships, although a rare site, do still exist today. They are almost all of the non-rigid type, or "blimps", with the exception of the contemporary Zeppelin NT, which has a modern semi-rigid type envelope. They are mainly used for advertising, survey, and film and TV work, as steady aerial camera platforms.

One last historical airship requires mention, from a steampunk standpoint – it was mentioned previously that non-rigid airships were used by the allies during the second world war to scout for submarines. The Goodyear blimp *Resolute* was one of a number commercial blimps purchased by the U.S.

Navy for use in a maritime patrol role. It was rumoured at the time that, as the vessel was being used for military reconnaissance *before* being officially commissioned in the U.S. Navy, that she must have been issued with an archaic "letter of marque" - essentially a license to commit piracy. While the exact legal considerations surrounding this are complicated (no letter was in fact issued, and her status as a privateer seems dubious from a practical standpoint), she, and the other Goodyear ships - used by the coastguard in a similar context - provide the closest historical analogue to bonafide airship pirates.

So where does that brief history leave us with regards to steampunk? Firstly, it's worth mentioning that there is much, much more to that story than is repeated here – many more great names, achievements, impractical machines, and heroic deeds. It's difficult to do justice to the subject in such a short space – but the real world history of the airship isn't the main purpose of this book, and we must leave it there.

Secondly, it can be seen that the airship achieved far more in the 20th century than in the 19th. This could, in the minds of some, present an issue for steampunk – many of the illustrations on steampunk book covers and the like show rigid ships airships flying throughout the 19th century. Of course, steampunk is by its nature anachronistic – if we didn't mix and match elements of different historical eras, it wouldn't have the appeal that it does. Given that airships are so key to the genre and subculture, they make a good illustration of the issues with trying to set strict historical time limits on what is and what isn't steampunk.

PHYSICS OF FLIGHT

So far, we've discussed a number of historical ships, with some detail given on their construction – but before we proceed with a full discussion of how they fly, it's worth taking a detailed look at the three main types of airship: non rigid, semi rigid, and rigid.

Non rigid airships, also known as pressure ships or blimps, are the simplest type of airship, and the dominant type in use today. Like a party balloon, the shape of the ship is maintained by the pressure of the gas inside, which is kept slightly higher than atmospheric pressure. To account for changes in air pressure, (due to shifts in weather and temperature) a secondary balloon, called a ballonet, is positioned inside the main balloon, or envelope. This can be filled or emptied of air, to keep a roughly constant pressure inside the ship.

Semi rigid airships, as the name implies, sit somewhere between blimps and rigid ships. The shape of the envelope is still maintained by the pressure of the lifting gas, but the ship also incorporates a structural keel. This helps spread the weight of the gondola and engines evenly across the envelope and enhances the structural strength of the ship.

At their simplest, rigid airships are an aluminium, or occasionally wooden frame, with a tight doped canvas stretched cover over. A series of gas cells, containing hydrogen or helium, are arrayed inside, and power is supplied by a series of engine cars on the outside of the framework. Unlike non-rigid airships, no ballonets are fitted - instead, the gas cells are made of goldbeater's skin, aka cow intestines (rubberised silk was used later on), which is impervious to hydrogen. As the air pressure changes around the ship, the cells can expend and contract to an extent. To cope with more extreme changes, relief valves can vent to account for very high pressures, and ballast may be dropped if the gas becomes cooler and denser to make the ship lighter again.

It's worth mentioning as well that monocoque and semi-monocoque, metal skinned ships have also been tried – these are technically rigid airships, but resemble blimps in appearance. Here, the skin of the envelope is made of thin sheet metal, usually an aluminium alloy, and gives the vessel its strength. Some lightweight support structure may also be included inside to help stiffen the skin. ZMC-2, an interwar U.S. Navy ship, provides the best example of this type. Interestingly, the first vessel of this type actually flew in the late 19th century – the Austro-Hungarian engineer David Schwarz designed an aluminium skinned airship that flew in 1897. The ship was destroyed a few minutes into its first flight however – the seams between the aluminium sheets making up the envelope leaked and the vessel crashed.

So the next key question – how does an airship actually fly? The answer lies in Archimedes principle, which rather drily states that to float "an object must displace a mass of fluid equal to its own mass". Although true, this isn't very helpful when first thinking about airship flight. There are, happily, other ways of thinking about it which may be easier to understand.

Airships fly in exactly the same way that a surface ship floats. What a surface ship is doing, when it sits in the water, is pushing water aside – naturally, the water pushes back, and it is this reaction force, called upthrust, which supports the ship and stops it sinking. If the upthrust force equals the weight of the ship, then it will float. If not, it will sink.

Surface ships, of course, are very heavy objects – generally made today of steel. The mental trap that people fall into is that steel is too heavy to float – which is true – but they forget that the ship is mainly full of air. When taken as a total, the weight of the steel, and of the air below the waterline of the ship, will be equal to the weight of the water that the ship is pushing aside – and here we have Archimedes principal.

Put another way – imagine making a simple boat out of household tin foil. "Tin" foil is actually aluminium, and is clearly denser than water. The boat however, will float. Now take that boat and crush it right down into a ball – and it will sink. Beware however, if you try this at home – you really have to get all of the air out of the tin foil ball. The author has fallen foul of this during a demonstration previously!

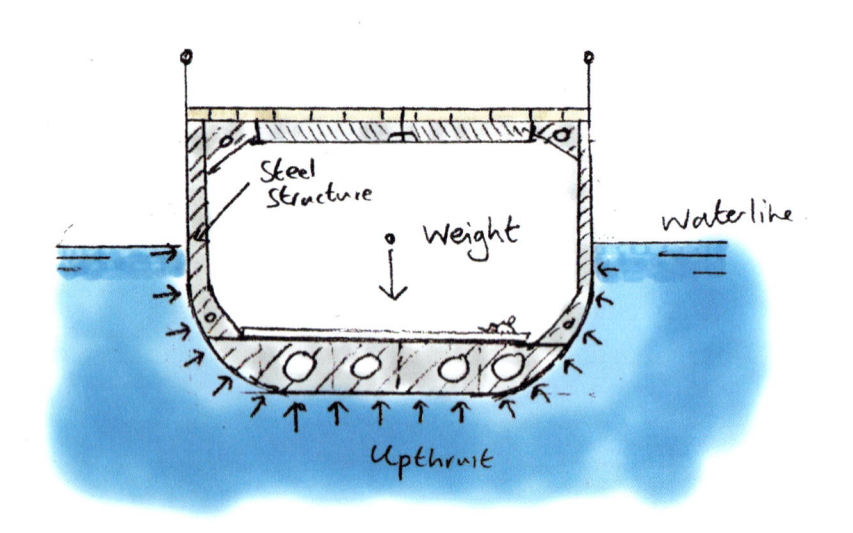

For an airship, things work in exactly the same way. The envelope or gas cells are filled with a lifting gas, typically hydrogen or helium, or for thermal airships, hot air. This has to be less dense than the surrounding air.

The problem then with airships is that you don't get very much lift - hydrogen and helium are less dense than air, but not by much, so you get very little upthrust force compared to a ship floating on the sea - the air inside a surface ship is about a 800 less dense than seawater; for an airship, the difference is more like 8 to 13 times less dense (for helium to hydrogen). You can see from this that you won't be able to lift very much, unless you have a really large airship. This is why rigid airships became so popular – the internal framework allowed the construction of substantially larger vessels than the largest non-rigid types of the day.

Weight therefore presents an issue for steampunks - all those engines, armour plates, rayguns and the like just wouldn't be feasible without a better lifting gas. Sadly, you can't go lighter than hydrogen when it comes to real world lifting gases. Vacuum airships are theoretically possible, and would generate the greatest possible lift for a real world vessel – however, a very strong and light material would be required to construct a rigid cell to contain the required vacuum, and withstand atmospheric pressure.

PRESSURE HEIGHT

One issue which must be considered in airship flight is what's known as pressure height. Air pressure is not constant – it decreases as a ship increases its altitude; likewise it changes with weather. Stormy, rainy days are typically linked with low pressure, whereas bright, hot and sunny days tend to be a symptom of high pressure.

The lifting gas in an airship will increase in volume as the ambient air pressure around it drops. It will also change volume with temperature – hotter gases increase in volume and become less dense; this is why hot air balloons work, as the warm air inside is slightly lighter than the surrounding air.

This is the reason for a ballonet on a non-rigid ship – as the lifting gas changes in volume, the ballonet can be filled and emptied to maintain a constant pressure. On a rigid vessel, where no ballonet is fitted, care has to be taken not to let the lifting gas within the cells expand too much. If it does, if will have to be vented off to avoid bursting them.

This presents an issue for the aerial mariner. If a ship flies too high, into lower density air, the lifting cells will have to be vented. If a large amount of gas is vented, there may not be enough gas left to maintain the shape of the cells at lower altitude where the air is denser, and the ship will sink and crash if it can't drop enough ballast to recover.

STABILITY

With any ship, stability is a key issue – floating is one thing, but floating the right way up quite another. Airship stability is simple and very similar to that of submarines, but quite distinct from that of surface ships – the process there is much more complicated, and involves the interaction of the centre of buoyancy, centre of gravity and what is known as the metacentre.

On an airship or submarine, only two factors come into play – the centres of gravity (CoG) and buoyancy (CoB). The centre of gravity of an object is the point through which its weight acts – its balancing point, in other words. The centre of buoyancy is the centre of the volume that's displacing air and generating upthrust – for all intents and purposes, it'll be close to the centre of the envelope.

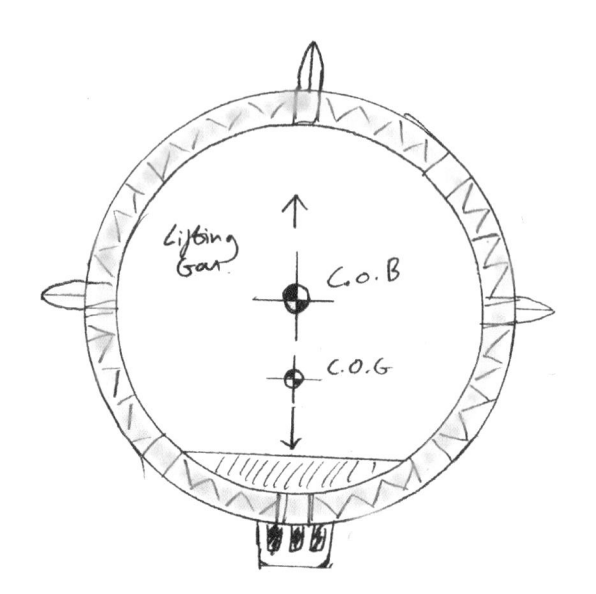

To stay upright then, all that needs to happen is for the centre of gravity to be below the centre of buoyancy. This is the reason why the gondola of an airship is always underneath, and the vast majority of internal accommodation on a rigid airship is to be found either in the gondola, or along the bottom of the ship.

PROPULSION

The feature that separates the airship from the free balloon is the the ability to steer the ship, or make it dirigible – i.e. the engine and propellers.

A number of engine types have historically been used on real world airships – steam, electric, petrol, diesel, and gas. Human power (oars, hand cranked propellers) and sails have additionally been tried, but without success. Of these, the internal combustion engines were the most successful, although petrol engines were frowned upon by some parties due to the potential for stray sparks to ignite leaking hydrogen.

One sail based experiment did try to address the issue of the lack of a keel – the *Eagle* balloon of 1897. The balloon used in the Arctic expedition was equipped with a drag rope, hanging under the balloon and trailing along the ground behind, in an attempt to make the sail-equipped balloon steerable.

This proved ineffective however and the balloon could not be steered. The expedition came to a tragic end shortly after it began – the *Eagle* crashed a few days after setting off. The occupants survived the initial crash but died of exposure while trekking back towards safety. Interestingly, photographic film of the expedition survived on the ice and was recovered in 1930.

It's probably worth adding here a short description of the different types of steam engine, and how they work. In general terms, there were two types used in transportation – reciprocating engines and steam turbines. In both types, steam is generated by a boiler – initially these fired by coal, charcoal or wood, but oil was used as well in later years. Fundamentally, anything that produces heat can be used to fire a boiler and drive a steam engine – today, nuclear reactors provide a very modern example.

Reciprocating engines are the earlier type (in the modern era), and use the steam pressure to push a piston. Steam is fed into the cylinder; this expands, pushing down on the piston. This movement is used to turn a crankshaft, producing the rotary motion needed to turn a wheel or propeller. Many variations exist on this engine type, but marine engines by the end of the 19th century were typically compounding or triple expansion types – using several cylinders and pistons to get as mechanical energy as possible out of the steam

The steam turbine was invented by Charles Parson in 1884, and is still in widespread use today. These use much hotter steam – what is know as "dry" steam – to directly turn one or a series of turbines, much like a windmill or wind turbine. Internally, an impulse steam turbine superficially resembles a jet engine, a.k.a a *gas turbine*. The turbine blades themselves are relatively small, with many tens arrayed around each rotor (wheel). Several rotors are used in sequence to get as much work as possible out of the steam. We often (erroneously) think of steam engines as being antiquated, slow moving affairs – not so with the steam turbine; these can be seriously powerful machines, with the shafts spinning at speeds of 3000rpm and higher. To the author's knowledge, no steam turbine has ever been installed on an airship.

From a steampunk standpoint, a steam powered airship is clearly the most tempting – but it's worth noting as well that internal combustion engines were around in the mid to late 19th century, and it's an interesting "what if" to imagine some enterprising engineer fitting an early gas engine to an airship in the 1860's. Maybe Giffard would have been more successful? Maybe we could have seen the first aerial battles during the American Civil War, or the first passenger flights across the channel?

The Fictional Airship – Classifying the Impossible

In the previous two chapters, we've had a look at the real world history and physics of airships – this is where we depart into the purely fictional. A knowledge of the real world is still important however – fictions are usually more convincing if they have some basis in fact.

Unlike their real world counterparts, steampunk airships do not fit neatly into pre-defined classes. In fact, to the author's knowledge, no one has yet tried to define steampunk airships thus – so perhaps its time someone made a start and tried, for the sake of illustration, and to provide context to the subject as a whole. As physics is often out of the equation (so to speak), and each ship is individual to each artist or author, the "defining" factors shall be along the lines of aesthetics and general character.

In addition, there are two overarching categories which compliment the classes given below – those airships which fly by becoming lighter than air, and those which use other means to generate lift. The former tend towards the more realistic and the latter towards the fantastical, but this isn't always the case.

Of course, the aim here isn't be be prescriptive – it doesn't matter if a ship fits into more than one category (most of them do), or none of those mentioned – but hopefully, this will help break down and make the subject of steampunk & dieselpunk airships more accessible.

THE DREADNOUGHT

Named for the revolutionary HMS Dreadnought of 1906, The first of our classes includes the heaviest of the steampunk airships – usually with only a nod to physics, the flying dreadnought bristles with arms and armour, and echoes the great battleships of the late 19th and early 20th centuries.

The exact methods that keep these vessels airborne, but usually include exotic materials such as Liftwood (from the role-playing game *Space: 1889*), or a magnetic field to stay aloft. Some may also employ more traditional methods of generating lift, but with disproportionately small gas cells or envelopes.

Examples include - Herr Doktor's scale model *Leviathan,* the Royal Navy ships of the RPG series *Space: 1889*, The larger ships of the anime *The Last Exile*, and some of the heavier vessels in the online video game *Guns of Icarus*.

THE FLYING SAILING SHIP

The steampunk flying ship comes in two distinct flavours – the literal flying ship, and more traditional airships equipped with sails.

This idea has some real world pedigree – sails were tried repeatedly to make free balloons dirigible, but without success. Lacking a keel in the water to counterbalance the force of the sails, a real world sailing airship is doomed to drift with the wind – still, they represent an aesthetically pleasing class of steampunk airship, evoking the golden age of sail, and are a firm favourite of the author's.

With regards to the flying ship type – possibly the most well known examples are the spaceships in Disney's *Treasure Planet,* but they have made appearances through fiction for centuries.

A quasi-historical example of a literal flying ship is the mythical ghost ship the *Flying Dutchman* – she was at times reported seen flying above the horizon; likely the effect of a type of optical illusion acting on an actual sailing ship hidden by the curvature of the Earth.

More classic sail equipped airships have a been a common sight in steampunk for some time – typically, they are seen with variations on traditional sailing rigs, or auxiliary sails scattered across the envelope. Several examples are the creation of Myke Amend, the artist behind the band Abney Park's ship ~~HMS~~ *Ophelia*.

Modes of flight vary substantially between these vessels, as the type often overlaps with others – the Martian vessels of *Space: 1889* use "liftwood" like their European counterparts, whilst those in the *Edge Chronicle* books use rocks at first to generate lift. Sail-equipped airships tend to use a more traditional lighter than air theme, such as those in the *Guns of Icarus,* which feature varying numbers of aesthetic sails.

Examples include Treasure Planet, The Edge Chronicles, ~~HMS~~ *Ophelia*, the Martian ships of *Space: 1889,* the video game *Skies of Arcadia,* and numerous vessels in *Guns of Icarus.*

FLOATING ISLANDS

While not ships in the classical sense, floating towns and civilisations add charm and character to many fictional worlds. They serve as an analogue to the space stations found in space operas, or the havens of pirate fiction.

The grandfather of them all is Jonathan Swift's flying island *Laputa*, from his 17th century book *Gulliver's Travels*. This provided the inspiration for the island of the same name in studio Ghibli's 1986 film, *Laputa: Castle in the Sky.*

Some aerial cities, such as *Colombia* in the video game *Bioshock: Infinite* use balloons and rotor blades to fly, while others, such as *Laputa* itself, use a lodestone to explain their floating – a type of strongly magnetic rock.

Floating islands are also featured in many fantasy works, and provide a link between steampunk and fantasy. Their often magical nature makes them a common sight in some of the more surreal sequences of games and films, such as the game *The Elder Scrolls V: Skyrim*. They are also a regular feature in classic fantasy art – the artist Roger Dean has made frequent use of them in his paintings.

Examples include *Laputa: Castle in the Sky*, *Mortal Engines* (Airhaven), and *Bioshock: Infinite*.

ROTORCRAFT

Using helicopter style rotor blades as the main or auxiliary means of flight is another common theme with fictional airships. Going back to the late 19th century, the *Frank Reade* stories featured several of the type, as did Jules Verne's books *Robur the Conquer* and *Master of the World*. Both Verne novels were combined into a film adaptation in 1961. More recently, they have made appearances in *Laputa: Castle in the Sky (*providing additional lift to the *Goliath),* and on the *Kirov* airships in the *Command and Conquer: Red Alert* video game series.

Compared to other fictional airship types, the rotor blade supported vessel have a common flaw – range; the majority of the other types - either by fictional or realistic - can remain aloft without using any fuel, whereas rotor blade based craft are constantly fighting the air to remain in the sky.

Interestingly, a helicopter-airship hybrid was tried in 1986 – the Piasecki PA-97 combined a U.S. Navy blimp with four Sikorsky H-34 helicopters. The aircraft was destroyed in a crash the same year, sadly killing one of the pilots.

Examples include - *Jules Verne's Robur the Conquer* and *Master of the world*, the *Command and Conquer: Red Alert* games series, the *Frank Reade* series of stories, and the PC game *Rise of Legends*.

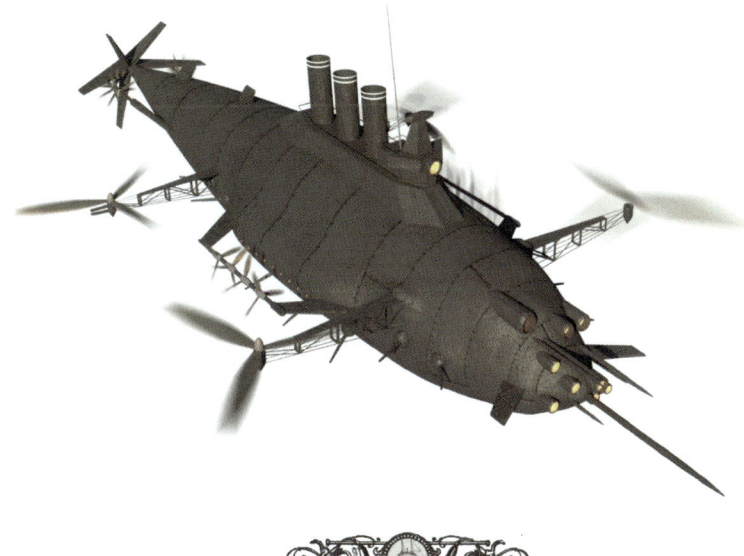

THE REALISTIC AND THE CLASSIC

Many steampunk airships designs have followed a relatively realistic theme, using minor visual variations to make fictional counterparts to real world blimps and Zeppelins. That's not to say all of these designs could actually fly – merely that they're based at least loosely on actual dirigibles.

It's difficult to pin down particular examples, as many steampunk books merely describe their airships as, well, *airships,* stating only a particular colour or minor aesthetic feature. This shouldn't be taken as a criticism of these vessels – they tend to suite their worlds very well indeed - but we've already covered the world of real airships in reasonable detail, and it would be pointless to repeat again here.

Chris Wooding's *Ketty Jay,* from his tales of the Ketty Jay book series fits into the "classic" category – the ship representing a good, solid steampunk airship with its own unique character and style, acting as much as a character in the books as a ship. The vessel using the fictional gas "aerium" to fly. This is a common theme used on fictional airships to explain the heavier nature of the vessels compared to their real-world counterparts.

As well as more outlandish vessels, the *Final Fantasy* series of games commonly feature airships, many of a classic type.

To give an example of the realistic type, the ships in Philip Reeve's *Mortal Engines* series fit into the realistic category. The artist David Frankland's cover to the second book, *Predators Gold*, gives an excellent view of the Jenny Haniver, the crimson enveloped ship flown by the protagonists.

Examples include – *Ketty Jay* (*Tales of the Ketty Jay* series), *Aurora* (*Airborn* by Kenneth Oppel), *Jenny Haniver* (*Mortal Engines*), various vessels from the *Final Fantasy* series of games.

MULTIPLE BALLOONS

Really a subset of other types, these are airships that have two or more envelopes providing lift, usually side by side or with one above the other. This feature can be found right across the range of steampunk ship types, with the exception of those that don't use lighter-than-air principles to fly.

HANGING BOATS

Again a subset of the realistic and generic type, these airships feature a boat or ship slung underneath a traditional airship envelope. The type and size of under slung ship varies, from the 17th men of war found in the 2011 film adaptation of *The Three Musketeers,* to the battered trawler-esque vessel in the 2007 film of Neil Gaiman's novel *Stardust*.

Early real world airships did in fact make use of this configuration – gondolas often resembled boats (such as on the British airship *Beta*), and most early blimp type ships had their gondolas suspended by cables below the envelope. This helped ensure that any flames or sparks from their engines remained well clear of the hydrogen lifting gas above.

Examples include - *The Three Musketeers* (2011), and *Stardust* (2007)

AERIAL AIRCRAFT CARRIERS

As much a dieselpunk craft as steampunk, The descriptively named flying aircraft carriers act as a mother-ship for smaller airships or heavier than air craft, such as biplanes or ornithopters. They come in a variety of forms, some with flight decks on top of airship envelopes, and some with internal hangars.

The real world rigid airships USS *Macon* and USS *Akron* fitted into this category, with their compliment of F9C Sparrowhawk fighters. Fictional examples include the *Tigermoth* from *Laputa: Castle in the Sky,* and the *Silvana* from the anime *Last Exile*. The former carries another staple of steampunk flight – the ornithopter ("Flappters") in a hangar slung under the gondola.

Examples include - *Silvana (Last Exile), Tigermoth (Laputa)* and the real world R33, USS *Macon* and USS *Akron*.

FREE BALLOONS

While not true airships, unpowered free balloons (such as hot air balloons) appear frequently through steampunk fiction – a fine example graces David Frankland's cover of *Mortal Engines*. Balloons also notably appear in the book *Ragged Astronauts* by Bob Shaw – here they permit flight between two worlds sharing a common atmosphere. "Hybrid" type airships are also a common feature in artworks – dirigibles that use a classic spherical shaped balloon rather than the more classic cigar shape more usually seen.

More bizarre variations incorporate sea creatures into their designs – in *Perdido Street Station* by China Mieville, floating Man-o-war Jellyfish are used for riot control by the draconian government.

Any society that can build a lighter-than-air airship must by extension be able to build free balloons as well. For those of us in the real world, they remain the most accessible means of experiencing lighter than air flight.

THE OUTLANDISH, THE LIVING AND THE MAGICAL.

Even given the range of types given above, some fictional airships defy stricter classification – generally, these are airships of a very unique character or appearance. To give an example, the airship *Fahrenheit* in the game Final Fantasy X fits well into this description – the means of flight and propulsion are mysterious, but the vessel works well in its stylised setting.

Many fantasy worlds also include "airships" which fly through magical means, but are hard to classify – a variety of examples can be found in artwork on the playing cards of Wizard's of the Coast's card game *Magic: the Gathering.*

Living airships could also fit into this group – Scott Westerfield's book *Leviathan* features airships built around flying whales, while airships built around fish-shaped envelopes appear frequently in steampunk artwork. Marine creatures remain a common staple for this type of vessel.

The Air Kraken (*Architeuthis Aeronautic*), another steampunk favourite, also belongs here – although by no means an airship, these flying cephalopods remain a common trope throughout steampunk fiction. The means by which air kraken fly varies, but tend to feature bladders of lighter than air gases, or wings. Either way, they present a severe danger to the aerial mariner. They do, strangely, have a real world counterpart – the flying squid.

Examples include – various vessels from the *Final Fantasy* Series of games, the Martian airships of *John Carter* (the 2012 Disney Film), and *Leviathan* (Scott Westerfield book).

NOTES ON DESIGNING STEAMPUNK AIRSHIPS

Steampunk is very much an interactive sub-culture, and it's very likely that those of you reading this book have an interest in creating your own airships, either in print, on paper, or in model form. In this chapter is given a rough design process that may be of use to those starting out – it can be difficult to know exactly where to begin, so hopefully this will help those interested create their first fictional flying machines. Some of the details given in previous chapters have been repeated here to help illustrate the points being made, the style of writing is a little less formal than previous chapters – the details are modified from lecture notes on a talk given by the author at the 2017 *Weekend at the Asylum* steampunk festival in Lincoln.

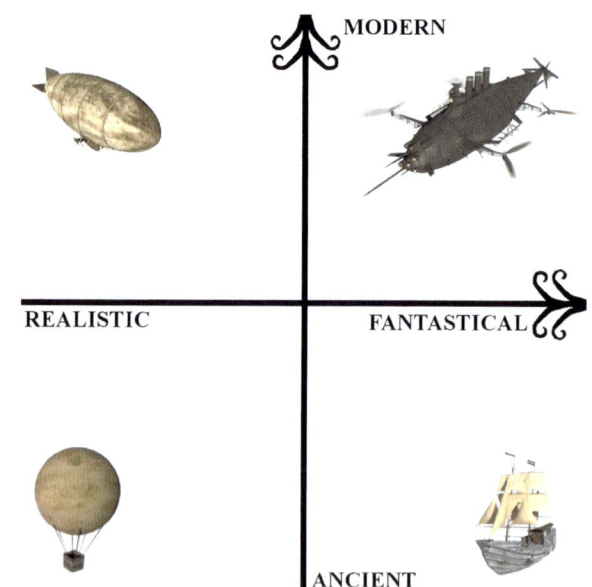

The scariest and most exciting thing in the design process is a blank piece of paper. Each step along the road gets progressively easier once you start to fill in the blanks, but getting moving is always the hardest thing. In a real world design, the very first thing you need to decide is exactly what sort of ship is needed. With steampunk, there's an additional pair of points to decide first – the world in which your fiction is set, and when.

For where, it's a question of how far you can push the laws of physics. At one end of the scale, you have the hard scientific – alternate history perhaps, but the laws of physics apply as we know them. At the other end, you have high fantasy – problems of science are brushed away and explained - sometimes literally - by magic, or by technologies so advanced or mysterious that they may as well be magic.

Additionally, steampunk can cover a wide range of historical periods, loosely from the regency era (*Powderpunk*) through to the late 1940's (*Dieselpunk*) – even without going even further with themes such as post-apocalyptic steampunk or steam fantasy. Of course, you can mix different eras together (something to be positively encouraged), but broadly these requirements can be plotted together to give sort of compass – so the first step is locating or deciding where you are on this chart, for your ship and

for the world in which it is set. Personally, I tend towards low fantasy – you can bend the laws of physics a little, but the designs still tend to be fairly realistic.

Next is deciding roughly what sort of vessel your airship is going to be – what role it was designed for or modified to fill; this will be heavily influenced by the time period, and the sort of "background" your ship comes from. Historical naval architecture can be a fine source of inspiration for this, treating airships as developments of surface going ships. Alternatively, you might take inspiration from vintage aviation – so your airship might be classed as a fighter or a bomber instead.

Using real world examples to begin with gives you a ready choice of ship class or type. For example, the vessel could be defined as a warship, specifically a corvette – so immediately, it's quite a small vessel, relative to other warships, lightly armed and armoured with an emphasis on speed. Historical examples of corvettes can be examined and design elements incorporated – for a vessel of say 1860-1870, that could be a combination of a steam engine and sails for propulsion, a small number of heavier guns for armament, and plenty of polished brass-work.

This gives a strong starting point – next comes the detail; design elements can be taken from pretty much anywhere – historical aviation is an obvious choice, along with architecture (think wrought iron), fictional spaceships, steam trains, and even nature. It's usually best, for a unique design, to mix several together – although with steampunk, it is also usually best to place an emphasis on historical styles to get something broadly in keeping.

It's worth noting that designing like this, it's up to you how much of each element is used; don't forget as well that you can play around with them – you don't have to copy the existing designs exactly; push and pull the shapes, put them in different arrangements and generally muck about with them until you have something you like.

Of course, you (probably) don't want a direct copy of an 1860's warship, although this approach can work. So other design elements need adding; a clear choice, for lift, is the usual airship envelope (balloon). So now the 1860's warship is combined with a 1930's rigid airship, like the *Graf Zeppelin*, creating something new and unusual.

How much you take from each source element is up to you – on this basis, you could end up either with a literal flying ship, or a more subtle combination between the two. It does help though to pull the strongest and most dominant elements from the point in time at which your ship is set. Sparsely using more modern or older elements is more striking from a fiction standpoint – as an example, having an

airship with a strong mid-Victorian background equipped with a laser cannon is quite striking from a fiction standpoint, and can say quite a lot about it's world.

A good reason, with steampunk, for starting like this is the origin of the genre itself – as steampunk draws very strongly on historical designs, the general aesthetic is to some extent more firmly set than other sci-fi and fantasy genres. Good advice to those starting out in fictional design is to start with the above process, and slowly bring in more unique features, or items from additional sources, as the design progresses. This comes back to the idea of the design spiral – start off with a basic idea and keep going back and refining it until you end up with a finished product.

A key point to highlight is suspension of disbelief – unless you very carefully produce a "hard science" design, chances are your airship wouldn't actually be able to get off the ground. The trick is then to give your ship the appearance of being airworthy – failure to do this will make it difficult to "sell" the design to your audience. It's a hard thing to quantify, but one strategy to look at real world airships – and try and keep to their general proportions if you want a realistic looking design.

It's up to the individual how fine you go with regards to detail – for a book, a rough outline might be enough, but for painted artwork or a model you might need to really go down to fine detail. A key point when it comes to adding detail is function – details should give the impression of serving a purpose on the ship, rather than just being there for the sake of it.

A final detail that you'll need to think about is colour. You may think that, as a steampunk airship, colour choices are limited to browns, brass tones, greys etc. as the major colours – however, this is not the case. For a start, the Victorian era wasn't all sepia, as we often think of it – people wore brightly coloured clothes; warships, were very often painted in light shades of white, red and buff. All that can be advised here is research – look at the colours and styles of the times, and don't be afraid to break outside of the typical steampunk palette. Colour will have a huge impact on the look and feel of your final design.

As a closing point with regards to design, consistency is very valuable in fictional designs. Steampunk is a science fiction genre – if you want an in interesting design, chances are you're going to break the laws of physics somewhere. One of the best ways to maintain suspension of disbelief is to be consistent - create altered laws of physics for your world by all means, but once you've got them, stick with them – it'll give your designs strengths and weaknesses and a three-dimensionality that'll be lacking if you just use magic or mysterious scientific processes all the time to explain everything.

ARMS AND ARMOUR

The idea of arming flying machines is almost as old as the concept itself – even going back to *Laputa* in Gulliver's Travels – itself by no means the earliest example - the residents threaten to use their airborne position to drop boulders on enemies below, or even crush them with the island itself.

Historical airships have also carried armaments – Zeppelins carried incendiary and high explosive bombs during the first world war; maritime patrol blimps carried bombs and depth charges, and machine guns were common across all types.

On the other hand, airships aren't as easy to destroy as many imagine – even hydrogen filled airships are relatively difficult to set aflame. In the case of the Hindenburg, it is likely that gas had been leaking for some time before the vessel caught fire, and therefore had ample opportunity to mix with the surrounding air - hydrogen must be mixed with oxygen before it can burn.

To give an example - during the first world war, British aeroplane pilots had, at first, serious trouble shooting down raiding Zeppelins - incendiary bullets and explosive ammunition were both tried by themselves, but it took a combination of the two to reliably set light to the raiding airships. The explosive rounds would have punched large holes in the fabric envelopes and gas bags of the ships, allowing the gas to mix freely. The incendiary bullets could then finally have set fire to the escaping gas.

The use of inert helium in place of hydrogen pretty much eliminates the risk of fire - although fuel tanks may still be vulnerable. During the 1990's, the British army tested the survivability of helium airships by riddling one with machine gun fire - as the pressure inside is only very slightly higher than atmospheric pressure, it took hours for the ship to sink. This contradicts somewhat the idea we have of a blimp just "popping" like a balloon!

With this in mind then, how best to arm and armour our fictional airships? Filling them with an inert lifting gas, real or fictional, is a good start. Adding armour is another obvious choice, although this will move away from realism (not always a bad thing) in the design – armour tends to weigh an awful lot, and it's unlikely that a heavily armoured airship could fly. Keeping the lifting gas in separate cells within would also reduce vulnerability, as could some sort of self sealing membrane around the cells.

Excluding the real world examples given, the opportunities for arming steampunk airships are pretty much endless, and vary greatly in different fictional worlds. Individual steampunks even tend to show great imagination, and display a bewildering array of different armaments at festivals and conventions. To name but a few, lightning throwing Tesla rifles, Gothic ray-guns, auto-cannon and old-

school nautical guns are all popular choices, as are weapons such as harpoon guns, rams, grenade launchers and flamethrowers.

The choice of weapon then comes down again to where and when an airship is flying – a raygun suits better a vessel flying over the Martian canals than a tiny scout-ship for Nelson's aerial navy. Steampunk also supports more outlandish, silly and whimsical ideas for weaponry. As an alternative, why not equip them with a net thrower to catch other airships?

Airship Pirates & Privateers

A key theme that can't be ignored when it comes to steampunk airships is that of airship piracy and privateering. Like the theme of freedom that draws us to ships and flying machines, piracy also represents an idea of liberty – albeit a dark one. In a dark and dystopian steampunk world, blighted by heavy industry, smog and destitution, the idea of rebelling and taking to the skies aboard a flying ship is just too tempting an an idea for many of us to resist.

Perhaps unsurprisingly, fictional airship piracy draws frequently draws upon the historical "Golden age of Piracy" during the late 17th and early 18th centuries. The vast majority of pirate themes & aesthetics used in western culture date from that period, although a few, such as walking the plank, likely originated in the brief resurgence in piracy following the end of the Napoleonic wars in the early 19th Century.

The term "privateer" may require some explanation for some. Essentially, a privateer is a legalised pirate, employed by a sovereign state in times of war to attack the merchant shipping of enemy nations. A document, known as a Letter of Marque & Reprisal, gave the captain of that ship legal dispensation to capture ships of prescribed nations. Attacking ships of countries not listed in the letter was an act of piracy – and in fact, many pirate captains started out as privateers, who turned their hands to the former after the end of a major conflict.

Privateering was outlawed by most nations in the 1856 Paris Declaration; however, the United States of America was not party to this – a factor that came back to haunt them in the civil war, which started a few years later. The rebel Confederate states employed privateers to attack union shipping in the early stages of the war, although later vessels such as the CSS *Alabama* were technically commerce raiders rather than privateers.

With regards to practicality, it's hard to say how airship piracy would work – much depends on the fictional world in which it's taking place. In Chris Wooding's *Tales of the Ketty Jay* series of books, pirates damage their prey and force them to land before boarding. As an alternative, harpoons or grapnels could be used to drag victims in, before swinging aboard onto the enemy's rigging. Some nerve would be required to achieve this – bearing in mind where the gondola is on most airships, the pirates would have to cover quite some distance to board at all!

HALCYON SKIES

The skies in which fictional airships fly are every bit as important as the ships themselves. The world in which something exists gives it context, and vice versa. To use a nautical example, a steam tug might been modern in 1895 – but a museum piece by 2018. The very fact that the tug still exists in 2018 however tells us two things about the world – that there has been an industrial revolution, and that people care enough about the past to preserve it. In the same manner, the steampunk airship draws from its world and feeds back to it. High fantasy airships imply high fantasy worlds, while their presence informs us about the world's inhabitants – that they have developed enough to build these ships, and they value them enough to spend the time and effort doing so.

Looking at the appearance of particular ships can also tell us something – for example, a sailing airship ship with its rigging *underneath* the envelope implies a world disconnected from the ground – landing is such a rare occurrence that engineers can disregard it when designing their vessels.

Moving onto the make-up and structure of our skies, and disregarding the ground below, two interesting factors can to be considered. These are the altitudes at which the the fictional airships typically fly, and the composition of the atmosphere. Temperature and air density both decrease as you get higher, so an airship operating at altitude requires a very light structure and warm clothing for the crew. On the other hand, ships operating closer to the ground can be a little heavier, with more lightly dressed crew.

Why is is this important for fictional ships? Mainly, it helps add character to both the ship and its complement. At lower altitudes, one might find a crew gliding over palm tree lined lagoons in tropical clothing, sporting pith helmets and hunting rifles. On the other hand, you might expect high altitude sailors to be hardened veterans, wrapped up warm in fur lined boiler suits, flying caps and goggles pulled close to their heads, doggedly pushing on to their objective.

Our second point related to the make-up of the sky. This says an awful lot about the world – for example, a sickly yellow smog filled sky, with pirates coughing into ersatz respirators, suggests a dystopian world, tainted by years of mining and heavy industry. Either way, or even with something completely different – considering the sky in which airship flies while designing it, or contemplating existing examples, adds flavour to the subject.

Steampunk Shipyard

Over the course of my interest and involvement with steampunk, I have created numerous airship designs of my own. Many of these exist (or existed) in the form of scale models, and many more as computer generated images – these have been used in various short films and artworks.

A selection of these designs and their origins are presented here, along with a short fictional history of each. They represent my own personal view of the steampunk airship rather than a cross section of the type as a whole – however, I hope they prove interesting to the reader and help to inspire your own designs.

MERCANTILE JUNKS

These peaceful merchantmen ply the sky roads between the distance cities of far Nippon and Cathay. Sails provide power when the winds are fair, but a pair of powerful engines can provide a burst of speed to escape summer storms and marauding pirates.

These vessels were originally created for a friend's project, which sadly never bore fruit. The brief was for an airship with an east Asian feel. I experimented at first with the classic battened lug sails that typify Chinese and other Asian Junks, but they felt a little too cliché, even given the brief. The hull of the boat that makes up the gondola was based on a sampan however, and the deckhouse was fitted with a sweeping pagoda style roof.

The sails that were used in the end were loosely based on those of another far eastern vessel – the Indonesian *Prau or Prahu*. The masts and rigging are, of course, bamboo and bamboo fibre rope. The braced curve of the masts was meant to imply a lightweight but strong structure – something that bamboo typifies. The ships are shown sailing downwind in the picture opposite, with their propellers still – it was envisaged that most of the sails would be furled when steaming into the wind.

The method of handing the gondola below the envelope is a little different as well – I wanted to use the "hanging boat" style of gondola to give the vessel an archaic style. However, I didn't want to use the ropes and rigging that are usually seen – so a braced bamboo structure was chosen instead.

The vessels are unarmed – it was intended that these would be purely mercantile ships. This implies that they're flying in a relatively peaceful, well policed world - although of piracy has never died out, even in the modern world, and the vessels could be readily adapted for use by pirates. The addition of a few bronze cannon and repeating crossbow would turn them into fearsome light warships, although their fragile construction means they wouldn't stand up long to concentrated return fire.

S/S Albatross

The crew of the air pirate "Albatross" preyed for years on the aerial shipping over the western seas. They met their well deserved fate at the hands of the screw-frigate "Marengo". Lured by a complicated ruse involving a bread-crumb trail of rumours and false leads, they were led into the badlands and trapped by the frigate. The ship was destroyed following a short chase.

Albatross was created for Tigermoth production's semi-official video for the American Steampunk band Abney Park's song *Airship Pirates*. The original inspiration for the design came from a model I built some years ago. The model was hurriedly built for an art exhibition, and was a very rough kit-bash (conglomeration) of existing model kits. Many components came from an airfix kit of a Soviet Petylakov Pe-2 bomber.

The ship was intended to have a very late era steampunk feel, bordering on dieselpunk. For this reason, a corrupted version of the Petylakov's camouflage was retained on some of the components. A sailing rig was added to tone the modern feel of the design a little, and to give it some height and complexity. Likewise, an older style of cannon was chosen at first to increase the anachronistic theme, although this was later replaced by a three barrelled Gatling cannon on the final version of the design.

With regards to configuration, the arrangement of the ship is quite unusual and unbalanced. The cruciform arrangement of the engines and outriggers was inspired by a number of interwar biplanes. The decision to place the superstructure on top of the tail-fin was an attempt to break away from the almost ubiquitous "envelope on top, gondola under" configuration seen on all real and many fantastical airships.

As the vessel was used in a music video, we built several small sets to aid in filming, including the small observation post that can be seen on top of the superstructure. This was the first time I'd built a full sized piece of a steampunk airship, and it was a rather satisfying thing!

The final look of the vessel is very striking, but I've never been entirely happy with it. Although it's a fictional design, it feels unbalanced, with too much weight on top and towards the aft end. However, the design still has its charms and I'm sure it's one I'll re-visit in later years – perhaps with some sails underneath as well to counterbalance those on top.

Q-Ship

Air piracy had become rife over the Brigantine sea since the end of the war, with hundreds of tons of cargo being lost yearly to a disgruntled mix of ex-privateers and out of work whalers. The companies' response was the Q-ship – a merchantmen manned by a crew of hardened ex-navy veterans, and fitted with a nasty hidden quick-firing gun. The ships would cruise the skylanes, masquerading as an unarmed freighter. When the unsuspecting pirates got within range, the cargo hold doors would slide back to reveal the gun – too late to flee, the corsairs were either destroyed or surrendered.

The third of my designs was inspired by the first world war concept of a Q-ship. As the short fiction above suggests, these were converted merchant ships fitted with hidden guns – there to attack enemy submarines and commerce raiders. The idea of using false flags or disguising one type of vessel as another is even older, but that's a history best told elsewhere.

As a converted merchant vessel, I wanted the Q-ship to have a slow and lumbering appearance. For this reason, I used a squared, slab sided design for the envelope – aerodynamically highly inefficient, except at low speeds. Likewise, the gondola is essentially a box – ideal for carrying large amounts of cargo, but not so much for cruising at high speed.

The engines of the vessel are supported away from the envelope on a pair of outriggers, and are fitted with large contra-rotating propellers. These were intended to be a retrofit by the company – extra power to chase surprise pirates when required, and to chase them down. The engines themselves are steam turbines, again giving quite a late Victorian/Early Edwardian feel to the ship.

One feature that may stand out is the light affixed to the end of the bowsprit. This was a small visual "Easter egg", inspired by the deep sea angler fish – these use a bioluminescent "bulb" on the end of a stalk to lure in prey.

Overall, I feel this design fits well into the "classic" steampunk airship archetype, and I'm quite happy with it – one of very few of my designs not to feature sails!

M/V *Storm Petrel*

Since the great air whale had begin to disappear from the northern skies, more and more desperate whalers had raised the black flag turned to air piracy. This wasn't as it was in the misty days of old, when buccaneers plundered the treasure ships of ancient empires – this was simple survival, with each ship taken representing a few more precious days of food and fuel.

Of course, the Brigantine Sea Company would hunt them down in the end – but surely it was better than to die in battle than to starve?

Storm Petrel, relative to the other designs here, is based upon quite a complex mix of different themes and ideas. Her heart and soul is that if a whaleboat. This was a small vessel, formerly a rowing boat but latterly a small steamship – which would be sent out from a whaler to harpoon whales and drag them back for processing.

Aesthetically, she has a variety of historical influences, with some marine biology thrown in for good measure. Her envelope is part shark and part Messerschmitt Me-262, itself famously shark like. The gondola is based on the original Flash Gordon's rocket ship, while the engines are inspired by those of the second world war era K-class blimp.

The older elements in the ship include the sailing rig – part schooner and part Caique, a traditional Ionian sea fishing vessel. The colours used were selected as being quite typically steampunk – browns, sepias, and iron greys. This was to counterbalance the modern elements in the design – I don't like using a high proportion of Victorian details on my airships; instead I take elements from across the 18th, 19th and 20th centuries and bland them together, hoping to achieve something in the middle. In this case, the intend was to create a vessel typical of a dystopian maritime world, around the 1880's 1890's – I believe I've achieved this, and *Storm Petrel* is one of the designs I'm happiest with.

Some of you may be surprised at the use of the prefix M/V (motor vessel) for a Victorian airship. I did initially intend to have the vessel powered by a steam engine – but as gas engines were in use (on land) from the 1860's, I thought I'd use something a little different in my alternative history.

IRONCLAD RAM

Heavily armoured, the protected airship was a true product of the industrial revolution. Developments in armour meant that the modern guns were no longer capable of defeating these vessels – so, like the Greek triremes of old, naval architects resorted to putting rams on their ships. Impressive enough on a surface ship, this was terrifying on an airship – several hundred tons of hardened iron & duralumin crashing towards you at 40kts was enough to shake even the most weathered airshipmen.

The design for this ironclad was one that came to me quite randomly one evening. The concept of the surface going ironclad ram (such as the CSS *Virginia*, HMS *Polyphemus* and the like) is an interesting quirk of 19th century ship design – however, I wasn't thinking overly of designing a steampunk airship version at the time. For this reason, the concept was quite elusive at first, but I managed to narrow it down after starting on the digital model for the rendering.

Like many of my other designs, the general silhouette of this vessel is a mix between curved, organic shapes and more brutal angular ones. The prominent ram prow dominates the look of the ship, and heavy artillery in a series of ball mounted turrets adds to the menacing feel.

It was not my intention at first to add a sailing rig to this vessel, but as ever, habit got the better of me. The main sails were inspired by Robert Fulton's *Nautilus* submarine of 1800. This tiny submersible featured a folding sail for navigation when surfaced.

Sails aside, the vessel is supposed to be powered by a pair of internal steam engines, linked to the propellers via driveshaft and gearbox. I imagine the inside of the vessel as being reminiscent of a classic Victorian steam ship – a mix of iron plates, glowing, infernal boiler room, and a grand triple expansion steam engine.

This vessel fits very much into a high fantasy setting – it's far too heavy in appearance to have any real pretence of being able to fly. The design is one that I might develop in time – I like the idea of a rusting, battered pirate version, well past its best, with tatty sails and daubed in arcane symbols.

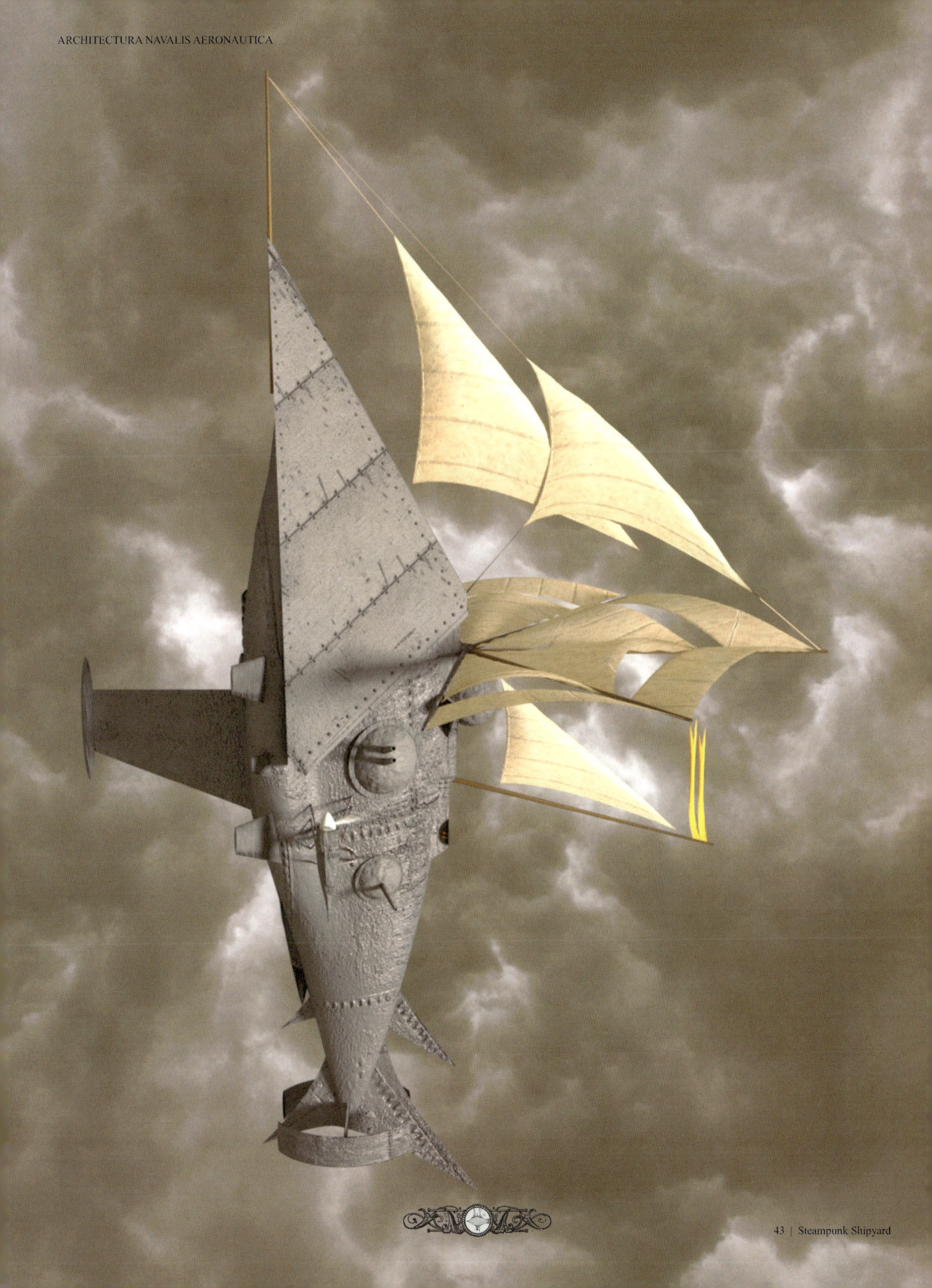

WINDJAMMER

Drifting through the low set clouds, merchant vessels were a common sight the world over. Although steam had largely taken over from sail, some antiquated shipping lines still preferred the old ways, and the sailing airship was still to be seen across the far flung reaches of the globe. Their low speed however made them easy prey for privateers and the occasional opportunistic pirate.

As the name and fictional history implies, this vessel was inspired by the last great sailing ships of the 19th and early 20th centuries. These vessels were known as the *windjammers*, and a very few remained in commercial service as late as the 1950's. Fuel, be it coal, diesel or heavy fuel oil, has always been a major cost in shipping – so using sails to propel your ship could be competitive historically, even in the days of steam.

Like the S/S *Albatross*, the requirement for this airship came from the music video we created for the band Abney Park's song *Airship Pirates* in 2016. In that video, we needed a lumbering merchant vessel that could be taken by our pirate "heroes".

The aesthetic design of the ship was based partly on a classic sailing barque, with the envelope shape stretched out underneath to represent a whale. One important feature was the large open deck on the stern of the gondola – this would give us ample space in the video for the pirates to board and take the vessel. On the gondola can be seen a fair number of portholes as well – these imply that the vessel is carrying passengers, helping to reinforce the helpless feel of the airship.

There are a fair number of sailing airships in this book, so perhaps it's worth mentioning here how I envisage the sails working. I've mentioned previously that you can't make a balloon dirigible (steerable) by adding sails as they lack any form of hydrodynamic keel to resist the force of the wind. My fictional solution is a lodestone – a magnetic stone that could interact with the earth's magnetic field and produce the necessary force, allowing you to steer the ship.

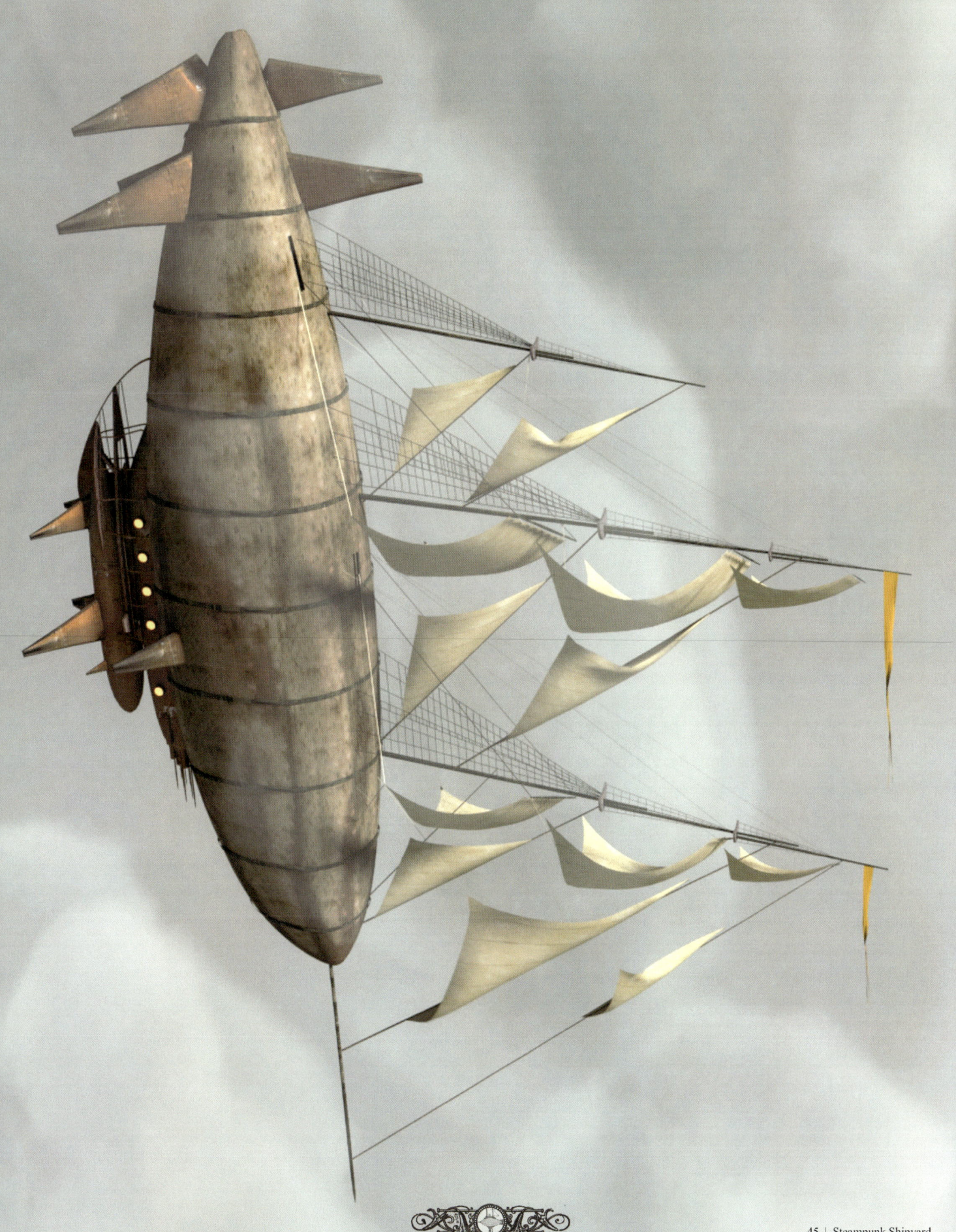

HAMMERHEAD SOUND WHALING STATION

Whale oil refineries such floating as that above the hammerhead sound are to be found dotted around the airlanes. As well as acting as processing plants for air kraken and drift-whale oil blubber – both key sources of lifting gas – they act as harbours and trading posts for myriad other aerial craft.

In recent times, due to the decline in the whaling, their leaders have had to turn to other means to stay in business – gambling, smuggling and piracy are rife now in many of these havens. The Navy takes a dim view of this of course, and the sight of a once thriving trading post burning into the night sky has become a sadly common one.

It seemed a shame to write a book on steampunk airships and not include at least a little slice of the worlds they fly in. As air piracy has been discussed throughout this book, a pirate haven and refinery seemed an interesting place to feature – the theme of whaling adds a dark, dystopian touch as well.

The look of the island upon which the refinery sits is based loosely on *Laputa*, in particular from the 1990's BBC adaptation of Gulliver's Travels. The rock itself is Welsh slate – I remember climbing Mt. Snowdon in heavy cloud some years ago, shortly after a steampunk festival. At one point, we found ourselves walking above the cloud, with only the cloud tops around us visible. The sensation of flying was very strong, and it's stuck in my mind ever since - providing inspiration whenever I create floating islands for steampunk worlds.

On top of the island sits the refinery and dock structure. Inspiration for this was from a variety of real-world industrial sites. I wanted to create the feel of a maze of buildings, gantries and pipework – all created from iron. The spherical building at the centre of the complex was added to give a slightly other-worldly feel – it could be many things, from accommodation, to gas storage, to something altogether more sinister.

One final touch is the horned *Isengard*-esque tower – a deliberate reference to JRR Tolkien's theme of dark satanic mills in *The Lord of the Rings*.